D0602953

# LAUGH-OUT-LOUD BABY

TONY
JOHNSTON

STEPHEN
GAMMELL

A Paula Wiseman Book
Simon & Schuster Books for Young Readers
NEW YORK   LONDON   TORONTO   SYDNEY   NEW DELHI

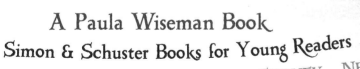

**T**he first time our baby laughed out loud
our family stood stock-still to listen.

That small spill of happiness
went rippling through the house—
a dazzle, a jazzle, a shine.
We all knew it was the sound of joy.
So we laughed out our joy too.

We picked up our jolly baby
and we passed him around.
Each one of us kissed him,
soft as a butterfly.
Each time we did, he laughed out loud.
So did we,

ALL JOLLILY.

Then I said,

"LET'S HAVE A LAUGH-OUT-LOUD PARTY."

So we did.

Everybody came.

OH, GLORY!

Aunts and uncles and cousins of all ages.
And crinkly grandmas and wrinkly grandpas.
And a throng of neighbors.

And our twinkly great-grandma,
who was old, old, old.

"I CAME TO LAUGH OUT LOUD," she said.

Then she GUFFAWED.

Everybody came jostling into the house
wearing smiling kinds of clothing.
They all entered, grinning and laughing,
because it was a laugh-out-loud party.

When they saw our merry little baby,
everybody scooped him up.
They looked into his shining new face
and smiled like pumpkins.
They coochy-cooed that baby cheerily
and tried to urge a laugh from him.

They tried with laughs of ALL sorts.

**SNICKERY NOSE** laughs
and **BELLY** laughs
and **DEEP DRUM** laughs
and THIN-AS-SKIN laughs
and **DOWN-TO-YOUR-TOES** laughs
and HORSEY **SNORTS**.

Until the walls of the house throbbed
with **HAPPINESS**. Our baby looked pleasant
as can be, but no laughs spurted from him.

So we passed around good foods,
both goopy and not.
Plates and plates.
Trays and trays.
Pots and pots.

And we got down to eating.
We ATE and we BLABBED.
And blabbed some more.

At last, when everybody was full of supper
and blab, there came along a slot of silence.
Like angels passing. And into that quiet
rang a little mirthful sound.

# WHOOPEE-DOODLES!

## OUR BABY

### LAUGHED!

So everybody erupted with mirth once more.
When they couldn't muster another **HEE-HEE-HEE**
or **HO-HO-HO**, the visitors said, "Aren't babies a
wonder?" Then they dwindled out our door.

They dwindled down the road,
some on foot, some on bikes, some in cars,
moving off into the dipping stars.
Before they went, soft as butterflies they kissed
our laugh-out-loud baby.
By then he was groggy with sleep.

But he must have felt those kisses,
because he smiled the sweetest smile.
He held his laughs inside himself—
until tomorrow.

For Noah, Yannik, Mallelai, and all babies.

May they know joy.

—TONY

From bear to baby and beyond.

Thanks always to Gertie and Chuck Geck.

—STEPHEN

For the Navajo, a child's first laugh has always been a precious moment.
They celebrate this event with a First Laugh Ceremony. The baby—with
the help of grown-ups—gives small, sweet gifts to each guest, so that he
will become generous; he gives nuggets of rock salt to keep him from being
stingy. Then, to bring good luck, the baby is passed from guest to guest.

SIMON & SCHUSTER BOOKS FOR YOUNG READERS • An imprint of Simon & Schuster Children's Publishing Division
• 1230 Avenue of the Americas, New York, New York 10020 • Text copyright © 2012 by Roger D. Johnston and Susan T.
Johnston, Trustees of the Johnston family Trust • Illustrations copyright © 2012 by Stephen Gammell • All rights reserved,
including the right of reproduction in whole or in part in any form. • SIMON & SCHUSTER BOOKS FOR YOUNG READERS is a trademark of
Simon & Schuster, Inc. • For information about special discounts for bulk purchases, please contact Simon & Schuster Special Sales at
1-866-506-1949 or business@simonandschuster.com. • The Simon & Schuster Speakers Bureau can bring authors to your live event.
For more information or to book an event, contact the Simon & Schuster Speakers Bureau at 1-866-248-3049 or visit our website at
www.simonspeakers.com. • Book design by Chloë Foglia • The text for this book is set in Windlass and Oklahoma. • The illustrations
for this book are rendered in a combination of watercolor, colored pencil, and pastels. • Manufactured in China
0612 SCP
2 4 6 8 10 9 7 5 3 1
Library of Congress Cataloging-in-Publication Data
Johnston, Tony, 1942– • Laugh out loud baby / Tony Johnston ; illustrated by Stephen Gammell. — 1st ed. • p. cm. • "A Paula Wiseman
Book." • Summary: The first time a baby laughs, his entire extended family gathers for a party in hopes of hearing the sweet sound
again. • ISBN 978-1-4424-1380-1 (hardcover : alk. paper) • (1. Laughter—Fiction. 2. Babies—Fiction. 3. Family life—Fiction. 4. Parties—
Fiction.) I. Gammell, Stephen, ill. II. Title. • PZ7.J6478Lau 2012 • (E)—dc23 • 2012006182 • ISBN 978-1-4424-3351-9 (eBook)

first
edition